Tip's Big Adventure

ISBN: 978-1-955531-56-6 (paperback)

Tip's Big Adventure

Tip's Big Adventure

DONNY HOLMAN

Once upon a time in a forest, far-far away from any humans, where only the strongest and smartest animals survive, there lived a pack of wolves. In this wolf pack, there was a momma wolf named Snow, who gave birth to a litter of wolf pups. In this litter, there was a runt named Tip. He was always trying to out do his brothers and sister, but never could.

One day Snow was left alone with her pups because Smokey, their father, went to find something to eat. Little did she know that she and her pups were being watched by Goosba, the grizzly bear, who was waiting for the right chance to attack.

just as Snow turned back, Goosba sprang into action
and knocked Snow out with one mighty blow.

When Snow came too, she realized that all her pups were dead except for Tip. Tip was nowhere in sight. Snow let out a terrible howl hoping that Tip or Smokey would hear her and come back fast. Smokey was in the middle of catching his family some food when he heard her howling and began to sense that something was terribly wrong, he ran back to where he left Snow. When he got back to her, he saw what had happened to his pups and asked Snow where Tip was.

She told him what happened with Goosba. Once Smokey heard the news, he grew angry but told Snow not to worry because everything would be okay. Hoping that Tip was still alive, they buried their pups and went in search of him, not knowing that Tip was only a few feet away, knocked out from the attack. When Tip woke up to find no one around, he got scared. So, he went in search of his family, not knowing that Snow and Smokey were looking for him too. Tip tried to put his keen sense of smell to work. He put his nose to the ground, and off into the night he went.

The sun rose early the next morning, and Tip had seen no sign of his family. Just when he decided to give up, he heard something in the distance, and that's where he saw his mother and father just as they were crossing the river.

He was so happy that he took off as fast as he could. He got to the edge of the river, started jumping and screaming for his mom, but accidentally fell in the river.

Snow stopped, looked back, and told Smokey she thought she heard something. They looked around but saw nothing, so they continued into the woods. They had no time to waste.

Tip began to panic as he was being swept down the stream. There was a waterfall ahead, so he knew he had to act fast. A hand reached out and grabbed him at the last second. Tip took a moment to catch his breath, then he looked up, saw a hyena, and said, 'Thank you, but who are you?" "My name is Solo," the hyena replied, "but what are you doing in the river?"

Tip told Solo how he had been trying to catch up to his family, fell into the river, and was swept down by the stream. He told Solo his name, thanked him for saving him, and told him he had to get going so he could catch up to his family. Solo said, 'Tip, I know this forest like the back of my paw, maybe I can tag along and help you find them." Tip said, "Sure, I wouldn't mind a little company, but where should we go first?" Solo told him, "I know an old buzzard named Scully that can help us, but it is a day and a half of walking away." Tip said, "Let's go," and they began their journey.

Once they arrived at Scully's, Solo yelled, "Scully, Scully, are you there? It's me, Solo, I need your help." Scully flew down and asked what the problem was.

Solo introduced him to Tip, told him about how he had been separated from his family. Scully flew high up in the sky and tried to see his family. Scully flew high up in the air and looked for miles and miles, but all he saw was a few elk, pigs, and Goosba. So, Scully returned to Tip and Solo to give them the bad news. Scully told them how he had only seen the elk, pigs, and Goosba. Then, he suggested that the two of them stay the night with him and get an early start in the morning. They agreed and begun to settle in for the evening. Solo asked Scully, 'Who is Goosba?" Scully told her, "Goosba is a big, bad bear. He has destroyed many families, including a family of coyotes. He has brought so much terror to the forest. But it is getting late, the two of you should get some rest. Goodnight, my friends."

Tip and Solo woke up early the next morning to continue their journey. They decided to go down into the valley, which was about three days walk from Scully's. Everything was going fine until they stopped to get a drink of water. They did not know it, but a mountain lion had been watching their every move for a while and waiting for a chance to make an attack.

When the mountain lion saw them getting a drink, he decided it was a perfect opportunity to make his move. He was about to pounce on Solo, but Tip leaped into action and pushed Solo out of harm's way. The lion ended up landing on Tip instead. He pinned him down and licked his lips as he was about to take a bite out of him. But luckily for Tip, Solo snuck up and bit the lion on the tail just before it was too late. It gave Tip a chance he needed to escape from the lion's grip.

Tip and Solo both begin to fight with him. Solo had him by the tail, and Tip had him by the ear. They both managed to push the lion in the river and sent him down the stream and over the waterfall. Tip turned to Solo and said, 'Thanks for not leaving me." Solo looked back at him and said, "You're Welcome. I would never leave my only friend; I knew the lion was there the whole time. I was waiting for my chance to pounce on him." Tip said, "Yeah, right, me too. I was going to take that lion, choke him, and turn him upside down!" Solo laughed and said, "Shhhh! Be quiet; I hear something."

They crept up to the sound and were amazed at what they saw. To their surprise, they saw a female wolf chasing a butterfly. Tip was curious, so he went up to her and asked what her name was. The female wolf said, "My name is

Mia. Who are you?" Tip smiled and said, "My name is Tip, and this is my friend, Solo. He has been helping me look for my family." Mia looked up quickly and said, "Is your mother's name Snow?" Tip was filled with hope and replied, "Yes, how did you know that?"

Mia said, "I met and talked with your mother and father a day ago. They were looking for you. They also told me what Goosba did to your family. I'm sorry to tell you, but Goosba killed all your brothers and sisters." Tip dropped his head and went to sit by a tree. Mia followed him and asked if he was okay. Tip said, "Yes, I will be okay. I'm just sad about my brothers and sisters." Mia told him, "It's okay. I know how you feel. Goosba killed my family too. I have been by myself for a long time. I think you should go find your parents. They are really worried about you. I know which way they went. I can help you find them!" Tip said, "Great!" Let's get along!" Mia said, 'The last place I saw them was at Sandy Hills." Solo jumped in and said, "I know how to get there! Follow me!"

Solo led them through the valley and toward Sandy Hills, but as they grew closer, something terrible happened. Solo fell and got stuck in some quicksand. He struggled and struggled to get free, but only sank deeper and deeper. Mia rushed to help her and said, "Grab a hold of my tail, and I will pull you out." She pulled and pulled until she realized she wasn't going to be able to pull him out alone. So, Tip told Mia to grab his tail and they began to pull together. They pulled and pulled, and finally pulled him out of the quicksand. Mia looked at Solo in relief and said, "Next time, you should be more careful and watch where you are going." Solo looked back and said, "Okay, I will. I knew it was there all along, though." Mia laughed and said, "Yeah, right. We better get going. I saw Tip's parent just a little further this way."

They continued their journey and eventually reached Sandy Hills. They went all the way to the top of the hill looking for them. Once they finally reached the top, Tip looked and saw his mother lying on the ground. He ran as fast as he could to his mother and saw that she was still breathing, but badly hurt.

18

He looked up and saw Smokey and Goosba fighting. The thought of his brothers and sisters ran through his mind as he began to run as fast as he could toward his father to help him. Tip surprised Goosba by jumping on his back and biting him on the neck.

Smokey began to fight even harder when he saw that his son was alive and had come to help him. Smokey and Tip managed to push Goosba down the hill and into the quicksand. Then they sat back and watched him from the top of the hill as he sank into the quicksand. Smokey said, "Son, I am sorry to tell you, but your brothers and sisters are dead." Tip looked up at him and said, "It's okay, dad. I already know. I'm just glad that you are okay." Then the father and son both ran to go check on Snow. They arrived to find Mia and Solo by her side, and that she was okay. They were very happy. Tip ran to his mother and gave her a big hug. Then he introduced Mia and Solo and told how they helped to find them. The sun began to set, and the moon came out. They were glad to be back together again, so they all began to look up at the moon and howl. Solo looked at them strangely and said, "It's a wolf thing." Then they all began to laugh together, like one big happy family.

The End

CPSIA information can be obtained
at www.ICGtesting.com
Printed in the USA
BVHW010352040123
655467BV00020B/783